W9-CPE-838

APR - - 2011

ANIMAL ANTICS A TO Z®

Polly Porcupine's Painting Prizes

by Barbara deRubertis • illustrated by R.W. Alley

THE KANE PRESS / NEW YORK

Alpha Betty's Class

Dilly Dog

Alexander Anteater

Bobby Baboon

Corky Cub

Hanna Hippo

Eddie Elephant

Frances Frog

Gertie Gorilla

Lana Llama

Izzy Impala

Jeremy Jackrabbit

Kylie Kangaroo

Maxwell Moose

Nina Nandu

Oliver Otter

Polly Porcupine

STAR
of the
BOOK

Quentin Quokka

Rosie Raccoon

Sammy Skunk

Tessa Tiger

Umma Ungka

Victor Vicuna

Walter Warthog

Xavier Ox

Yoko Yak

Zachary Zebra

EAST NORTHPORT PUBLIC LIBRARY
EAST NORTHPORT, NEW YORK

Text copyright © 2011 by Barbara deRubertis
Illustrations copyright © 2011 by R.W. Alley

All rights reserved. No part of this book may be reproduced or transmitted in any
form or by any means, electronic or mechanical, including photocopying, recording,
or by any information storage and retrieval system, without permission in writing from
the publisher. For information regarding permission, contact the publisher through its
website: www.kanepress.com.

Library of Congress Cataloging-in-Publication Data

deRubertis, Barbara.
Polly Porcupine's painting prizes / by Barbara deRubertis ; illustrated by R.W. Alley.
p. cm. — (Animal antics A to Z)
Summary: Polly Porcupine loves to paint, but she creates such
a mess that her parents do not know what to do.
ISBN 978-1-57565-337-2 (library binding : alk. paper) — ISBN 978-1-57565-328-0 (pbk. : alk. paper)
[1. Painting—Fiction. 2. Cleanliness—Fiction. 3. Porcupines—Fiction. 4. Alphabet.] I. Alley, R. W.
(Robert W.), ill. II. Title.
PZ7.D4475Po 2011
[E]—dc22   2010025289

1 3 5 7 9 10 8 6 4 2

First published in the United States of America in 2011 by Kane Press, Inc.
Printed in the United States of America
WOZ0111

Series Editor: Juliana Hanford
Book Design: Edward Miller

Animal Antics A to Z is a registered trademark of Kane Press, Inc.

www.kanepress.com

Polly Porcupine loved painting pictures.
She painted every day after school.

Polly painted BIG, close-up pictures.
And she used bright splashes of color.

She happily painted pictures of
LARGE pink petunias.
Of ENORMOUS purple plums.
And of GIANT red poppies.

Her paintings were colorful and creative.

But Polly was a very *sloppy* painter.
She would flip her paintbrush.
And drip paint. And spill water.

She even dripped and spilled on her
own paintings!

One day, *everything* went wrong.

Polly stepped in the paint.
Mama tripped over the water pot.
And Papa slipped on the drippy papers.

Oh, Polly!

"Oh, Polly!" said Mama. "Please clean up this mess! Then set the table for supper."

"But LOOK at my beautiful painting!" cried Polly.

"We'll look at it later," Papa replied. "It's too drippy now!"

Polly pouted as she picked strips of pepper off her pizza and popped them in her mouth.

"Why are you grumpy?" asked Papa.

"You don't appreciate my paintings," Polly replied.

"I would appreciate them more if they weren't so sloppy," said Papa. "Now cheer up! I made your favorite dessert—my perfect peach pie!"

"I don't like peach pie anymore," said Polly. If Papa didn't like her paintings, then she didn't like his peach pie.

Polly was still grumpy at school the next day.

"What's the problem, Polly?" asked her teacher,
Alpha Betty. "You look a little prickly today . . .
even for a porcupine!"

"I have a question," Polly whispered.
"Do you like my paintings?"

"Oh, yes!" said Alpha Betty.
"They are so colorful and creative!"

"Well, my parents think my paintings are
too sloppy," said Polly.

"Do YOU think they're too sloppy?" asked
Alpha Betty.

Polly sighed. "I guess. Maybe. Yes."

Alpha Betty smiled. "Polly, I've been planning
something that might interest you—
a class art show!"

"An ART SHOW?" Polly yelped.

"Yes," said Alpha Betty.
"Do you think you can paint a picture for it?
One that's NOT sloppy?"

"I can TRY!" said Polly.

Polly sped home after school. She presented
an invitation to her parents.

"Our class is having an ART SHOW!" Polly said.
"I need to start my painting right away!"

Mama and Papa looked worried.

"I will try really, REALLY hard
not to be sloppy," Polly promised.

Polly spread out newspaper.
She prepared her paints.
And she pinned up a piece of paper.

Then she dipped her brush in orange
paint and held it above the paper. . . .

"Oops!" Polly gasped.

A big, peach-colored splat plopped right
onto the middle of the paper!

"Oh, NO!" Polly cried.
"I've *already* ruined my painting!"

Polly pouted. . . . Then she pondered. . . .
And *POOF!* An idea popped into her head!

"I'll make something special out of that
peachy splat!" she said.

Polly painted quickly but VERY carefully.

She did not flip her brush.
She did not spill water.
When she dripped a drop of paint,
she stopped to wipe it up.

Polly had everything cleaned up
just before it was time for supper!

Then she *zipped* into the kitchen. She set the
table with plates, cups, spoons, and napkins.

Her parents were impressed . . . and curious!

"What did you paint, Polly?" they asked.

Polly smiled. "You'll find out at the art show!"

At school, Polly showed Alpha Betty how she
had fixed the problem with the splat of paint.

"Good job, Polly!" said Alpha Betty.

The morning of the show, Polly sprang out of bed.
She was VERY excited!

As soon as Mama and Papa were ready, Polly led
them to school . . . and right to her painting!

"Ta DA!" said Polly.

Mama and Papa were VERY surprised!
"Oh, Polly," they said. "It's perfect!"

For Polly had painted a picture of a HUGE
piece of Papa's perfect peach pie!

The painting wasn't drippy. Or spotty.
Or splotchy. Or sloppy!

Alpha Betty had given every painting a prize.
But Polly's painting had TWO prizes!

"What do your prizes say?" asked Papa.

Polly happily read her prize ribbons aloud.
"One says 'Most Appetizing Painting'!
And the other says . . . 'Neatest Painting'!"

Polly took the first ribbon and put it on Papa.
"I apologize for being so grumpy," said Polly.
"Your peach pie really IS my favorite dessert!"

Papa beamed. "And YOUR peach pie is my
favorite painting! I hope you feel very proud."

Polly Porcupine grinned.
"Right now I feel . . . HUNGRY!
Let's go home and have some peach pie!"

Art
Show
Today

And that is precisely what they did.

STAR OF THE BOOK: THE PORCUPINE

FUN FACTS

- Home: There are over 20 species of porcupines, and they live in every part of the world—except Antarctica.
- Family: Porcupines are *rodents*, like beavers, squirrels, and mice. Their name means "quill pig," but they are not related to pigs!
- Quills: If porcupines are attacked, they run backward toward their enemy, leaving the attacker full of sharp quills. Porcupines can raise their quills but can't actually shoot them!
- Size: Porcupines usually grow to be 2 to 3 feet long and weigh 15 to 35 pounds. But some have weighed as much as 60 pounds!
- **Did You Know?** Some porcupines can hang from trees by their tails!

LOOK BACK

Learning to identify letter sounds (phonemes) at the beginning, middle, and end of words is called "phonemic awareness."

- The word *pat* <u>begins</u> with the *p* sound. Listen to the words on page 8 being read again. When you hear a word that <u>begins</u> with the *p* sound, pat your head while you make one "puffing" *p* sound and then say the word!
- The word *clap* <u>ends</u> with the *p* sound! Listen to the words on page 21 being read again. When you hear a word that <u>ends</u> with the *p* sound, say the word and clap your hands when you pronounce the *p* sound!

TRY THIS!

Stand Up, Sit Down for P Sounds!

- Listen to the words in the box below being read aloud, one at a time.
- When you hear a word that <u>begins</u> with the *p* sound, stand up.
- When you hear a word that <u>ends</u> with the *p* sound, sit down.
- If you hear a word that <u>begins</u> AND <u>ends</u> with the *p* sound, stand up and then sit down!

> paint drip prize flip peep please
> hope plum pink stop pot drop pop

FOR MORE ACTIVITIES, go to Polly Porcupine's website at www.kanepress.com/AnimalAntics/PollyPorcupine.html
You'll also find a recipe for Polly Porcupine's Pretty Pepper Mini-Pizzas!